Also by Marguerite Vance

A Rainbow for Robin

A Rainbow for Robin

by MARGUERITE VANCE

Illustrated by Kenneth Longtemps

NEW YORK: E. P. DUTTON & CO., INC.

Second Printing January 1968

TO *Peggy Smith,*
WHO WAS THE INSPIRATION FOR THIS STORY

The author gratefully acknowledges the valuable information and advice received from Peggy's mother, Mrs. D. Alden Smith; her piano teacher, Dr. Jean Lord; and the conductor of the Phoenix Symphony Association, Guy Taylor.

A Rainbow for Robin

WHEN you read a story, do you wonder sometimes how the author happened to write it? I do, so I think before I begin writing this one I had better tell you how it all started.

One Saturday morning about six months ago, everything seemed to go wrong and I was cross. First of all, Meg, my sister, bumped into me hard on her way out of the house to meet some girls: Meg and I are always considerate of each other. My brother Mark teases me sometimes and we get into awful arguments, but Meg—never.

So when she came banging into me and then just hurried on after saying only, "Whoops, sorry"—

not stopping or anything—I was good and cross. Not that being bumped into is anything to get into a huff about. If we're playing tag or trying to do one of the Spanish dances with a lot of swishing around and stamping, of course we run into one another. Sometimes we even knock one another down, but that is different. It is just when I'm not expecting it and someone suddenly bangs into me, well—I guess it frightens me.

That was the first thing that made that particular Saturday morning bad. Then Mother had promised I could make pudding for lunch dessert, the kind that comes in a package and all you do is whip it up and plop a cherry on top of each glass. It's Daddy's favorite dessert. Well, the delivery boy forgot to bring it with the other things and then it was too late to get more, so I couldn't make it.

But worst of all was not going to the concert. Mother and Meg and Mark and I were going to hear the New York Symphony Orchestra play that afternoon. Daddy got our tickets over a month ago, and I had been counting the days. Then right after breakfast, Miss Blair, my music teacher, telephoned.

Something had gone wrong somewhere and the orchestra would not come to Canyon City until two weeks later.

I don't think I'm a crybaby, but those three things all rolled up into a ball inside me somewhere, and before I knew it, I'd curled up in the big chair by the window and begun to cry. The sobs kept pushing up and up and I couldn't stop them. Daddy once said that his grandfather told him, when he was a little boy, that the quickest way to be really unhappy is to be sorry for yourself. That Saturday morning Great-Grandfather Preston certainly would have been ashamed of me because I was so sorry for myself I thought I almost wanted to die.

Mother must have heard me, because she came in from the kitchen where she had been making an apple pie to take the place of my pudding. Mother never hurries or rushes at you or makes sudden jerky sounds that make you jump. When Linda Winthrup's mother comes over, she always bangs the door open and yells, "Hi, anybody home?" And when she laughs, it is like cups and saucers breaking. When Mother laughs, I always think of a little brook running over smooth, round stones.

She came over to me where I sat all scrunched up in the big chair and pushed my hair back off my forehead. "What's wrong, Bobbie?" she said. "I thought you were going over to Linda's. Mark said something about your rehearsing for the play."

I remembered then about the rehearsal and, I guess because I was so ashamed of having forgotten, it added one more thing to that unhappy morning and I cried harder than ever. I just couldn't stop. Mother sat down on the arm of the chair and put her arm around me, not saying anything but just waiting for me to get through crying.

At last she said, "Do you know something, Bobbie? I've been thinking. If we only knew all there is to know about the people around us, I'm sure we would have enough interesting material to fill many books. Now you, for example, could write a book all about yourself."

I blew my nose and uncurled my legs. "Me? But . . ."

"Yes, you could. I have a whole folder of things

you've written ever since you were a tiny girl. Some of them you said to me before you learned to write and I wrote them down for you. Why don't you begin—now, today—and write all about yourself, beginning as far back as you can remember? Then when you reach the present you can make it a sort of day-by-day diary. Think how interested other girls would be! And whenever you had a day like today, for instance, when things went wrong and you couldn't do what you had planned to do, you could always spend time with your book. Don't you think that might be fun?"

When Mother gets excited about anything, her excitement is catching. At first I hadn't thought I could write anything anyone would want to read, but now I wanted to begin. I felt a kind of Christmas–morning thrill begin to run all through me. I *knew* it would be fun!

Here is the way I began my book six months ago:

I'll begin with the family. My name is Robin Preston and in six months I'll be thirteen years old. There are five of us: Mother, Daddy, Meg—her real name is Margaretta for our Great-Aunt Margaretta Gaylord—Mark, and I. We live in the pretty little town of Carsonville in a house that Daddy says rambles like a winding river over flat country. It is all spread out on one floor, with a big fireplace in the living room and all the windows looking out on the garden and the faraway mountains. All around us are interesting places. There is an Indian reservation north of us and an Air Force base nearby, and you can just feel a lot of busy things going on around you all the time.

Daddy is an architect. Mark wants to be an architect, too. But, being Mark, he wants to learn everything there is to know right away. Mark never likes to wait for anything. Mother says his middle name should have been "Now" instead of "Norris." Even when we play duets on the piano, you can tell Mark is in a hurry because his notes get all mixed up with mine and we have to start over. He's a wonderful brother, though. Some of the best times I have are riding along on our tandem bike with him, singing "Old Macdonald Had a Farm" and for teasing me, I tease him about stuttering. When Mark gets terribly excited or mad at something, he stutters. For instance, he'll say, "Bobbie, you're a d-d-d-dope!" But before he gets to "dope," I say "d-d-d-darling," and I always add, "Oh, don't I know it! I'm a perfect d-d-d-darling. That's me." We usually end in a scuffle that starts us laughing and screaming until Mother calls, "Here, here, that's enough, you two! Stop it!"

Meg is a year older than Mark and almost three years older than I and in some ways she seems even older. She's tall and her hair is soft and crinkly. Her nose turns up a tiny bit and her skin is warm and soft. Her voice is low like Mother's, and when she laughs you do too because her laugh is so catching. Because she is older and has older friends than mine, we do not do many things together except sing and collect things. Meg collects clippings about girls who have won prizes in athletics—running, swimming, or tennis, things like that—and in her scrapbook she has a special section for girls from all over the world who won in the Olympic games last year. She is a wonderful tennis player herself. 15

I'll never forget a funny thing that happened one evening when we were washing the dinner dishes and it was her turn to dry. Doctor Baker, our minister, had had dinner with us that evening and I guess we were all a little on edge because he is what Mother calls hard to entertain. I had just washed and rinsed the small aluminum frying pan. Meg picked it up to dry, and as she so often does, she pretended it was a tennis racket and that she was whacking a ball with it. She went swish through the air, and somehow the pan flew out of her hand and hit a huge pile of aluminum cake tins and pie tins Mother had stacked on top of the refrigerator to give to the garbage collector the next day. They went flying in every direction, sounding as though we'd broken every dish in the house. The whole family came running, bringing Doctor Baker with them, and stopped in the doorway to see Meg standing in the middle of all those pans, so embarrassed that she wanted to crawl off and hide.

It was so funny that everyone began to laugh and Daddy said, when he could get his breath, "Well, when you have a budding tennis champion in the family, you can expect anything." It certainly did break the ice, and when Doctor Baker left, he was still chuckling.

Now that you have heard about the rest of the family, it is my turn. I forgot to tell you what I collect. I collect small glass things, tiny glass animals mostly, and I have a lovely little glass church with a steeple, and a red glass apple. But the thing that I love most in the world I don't collect: I just have it. It is music. The very first thing I remember was the tinkling sound coming from a music box that Mother held to my ear when I was a baby. I still have that music box and sometimes I like to take it to bed with me at night and, before I fall asleep, listen to its music. I see green forests with paths winding through them and at the end there is always a beautiful castle, and I go to sleep wondering who lives in that castle. Perhaps a whole family like mine, with a king and a queen for the father and mother, and a boy like Mark, and two girls like Meg and me.

And that is one of the most interesting things in the world, I think. I mean, that some of us live in 17

castles and some in houses like ours; that some are
fat and some are thin. Each of us is different: Mark
stutters sometimes; Meg doesn't like chocolate—
can you imagine that?—and the reason I love beautiful sounds so much, I guess, is because my way
of being different is that I am blind.

I remember as a baby sitting on Mother's lap at
the piano. I put my hand down on the keys and a
funny, mixed-up sound came out, but no tune. I
remember I didn't like the sound very much, but I
knew I wanted a tune—I mean, a clear sound. I put
one finger down and out came a clear, clean sound.
I tried other keys. Some sounded round and warm
like my glass apple when the sun has been shining
on it, some sort of rumbly like coffee percolating,
and some, those far down on the keyboard, were
just like thunder. And all together—if you touched
keys that made a matching sound—you had music!

I didn't discover all that in one day, but I do remember that after that first time I loved more than
anything else to sit at the piano and pick out the
notes that matched. Then one day a wonderful
thing happened: I found I had made a tune! After

that I listened to the tunes Meg's music teacher gave her and sang the tunes over to myself and then made them into real pieces myself, making the treble and bass notes blend together. I think I knew right then that what I really wanted more than anything else in the world was to make new tunes, beautiful tunes for other people to play and enjoy. I began taking music lessons with Miss Blair when I was six, and for my seventh birthday I got a metronome to help me with my timing.

Maybe I had better tell you before I go any further that I am writing this on my brailler, and that when I have finished it, I'll copy it on the typewriter so a sighted person can read it.

Although I love the piano, I don't spend all my time playing. Mother thinks all girls should know how to keep house, so before Meg and I leave for school each morning, we make our beds and put things in their right places. Saturday morning is cleanup morning. We change the sheets and pillowcases, run the carpet sweeper and floor mop, and empty the wastebasket.

We always have plans for the day so we usually

finish with our room by nine o'clock. Then Meg goes off to play tennis or sometimes she joins Mark and me on one of our favorite hikes over to the other side of town where Grandpa Preston lives.

Everybody ought to have a Grandpa Preston. It isn't only that he can tell the most wonderful stories about when his father was a little boy and Arizona was still called Arizona Territory and there were terrible Indian raids, but he makes the yummiest cookies you can imagine. You ask him what he puts in them and he will always answer, "Oh, just a little bit of everything that looks good and tastes good." The cookies are never the same twice. Sometimes there are a lot of peanuts in them. and sometimes they are full of dates and figs, or he'll decide to make anise cookies that smell like Christmas. You can smell them baking when you turn in at the gate. No matter when you go to Grandpa Preston's, there is always a big crock of cookies in the pantry. But Saturday is his baking day and, as a lot of other kids know about it, too, Mark and I like to get there early.

Afterward, I sometimes go over to Linda's. The Winthrups live just three houses away from us and I know my way there as well as I do around our living room. Linda and I like to play records and sing along with the songs, or we work on the afghan we're crocheting for the church fair. This is really fun because we're doing it in squares, using two colors—forest–green and copper–brown—and if we keep our promise to each other to make four squares every week, we should have it finished in plenty of time. We and the other girls in our Sunday school class are selling chances for it at ten cents a chance, and it is just wonderful how much we already have! The afghan should be ever so pretty when it's finished—like a piece of forest when the frost has touched some of the leaves—and we're working hard.

People are funny about some things. A girl we know, Bess Burgess, comes over sometimes to watch us work, and one morning when I was saying how pretty I thought the afghan was going to be, Bess said, "Why, Bobbie, how can you possibly know whether it's pretty or not? You can't see it."

Linda said, "Bess Burgess, aren't you ashamed of yourself?"

I knew why Linda was mad, but honestly I wasn't mad or hurt, either, only sorry a little bit for Bess because she doesn't understand. I don't think Linda does either, but she pretends she does to be polite, because we're friends, I guess.

Since this book is about me, I think you might like to know how I do feel about colors. I don't think about it very much, really, but it is so simple. If someone asked you to describe green or pink or blue, what would you say? You know each color has a name, but how would you describe it? Well, I know each color has a name, too, and it is just as plain to me as it is to you. I see it in many different ways.

For instance, from as far back as I can remember, white is the cold spray of the shower, and frozen white is snow or ice. White is the feel of smooth, cool sheets on my bed, and when I read that a flower or a girl's dress is white, I know exactly what it looks like. Green is the smell of the grass when Mark cuts it. It is the feel of the leaves on the cottonwood trees in our back yard. Pink is the spicy smell of carnations, the creamy, prickly taste of wintergreen candy. Oh, I know what pink is, all right. I think my way of knowing about all the colors is just as easy and just as true and just as hard to describe as your way of knowing. That is true about so many things. After all, doesn't each of us do things a little differently than anyone else? You see, being blind is only one of those differences.

I haven't told you about one of the most important members of our family—one of the dearest. She is a tiny dog, a Chihuahua, the warmest, most loving, most faithful little dog you can imagine. Daddy brought her to me on my seventh birthday; I'll never forget that day. I had had my party in the afternoon with a birthday cake and candles to blow out and paper caps and everything. The girls had just gone home when Daddy came in a little early from the office. He came over to where I was folding Mark's present, a pretty plaid ribbon for my pony tail, and he said, "Hold out your hands, birthday girl, and meet a new friend."

I wasn't quite sure what he meant, but I held

out my hands, close together as he told me, and in a second he had put into them a tiny, soft bundle that snuffled and squeaked a little and began sort of scrabbling up the front of my sweater. I knew I had a puppy! A darling puppy all my own. I had been wanting one for so long and now here it was. I just couldn't believe it.

The rest of the family clustered around, and Mark kept saying, "Gee, but isn't it cute? Isn't it the greatest?" And Meg and Mother stroked the little head where it was snuggled up under my chin. The puppy licked my chin and buried her head deeper into my neck and made me laugh, and I knew we had adopted each other. I tried to find words to thank Daddy, but all I could say was, "She's mine—she's all mine!" I decided to call her Perky because that's the way she felt, with her little ears perked up and her whole body just shaking with excitement and happiness at being with me.

That was five years ago, and since then Perky and I have never been far apart. She sleeps on my

bed and sometimes when I wake up at night, I find

her curled tight against my shoulder, just sleeping away so hard. You know—sort of snoring way down deep inside of herself.

Last year, for Daddy's birthday, I wrote a little piece that I called "Perky." It was ever so exciting because I had had to compose the piece and then memorize it when he was not at home, and I worried for fear I'd forget the little allegro part where I tried to describe Perky bouncing around the way she does when she's waiting for me to throw a stick for her to fetch.

It was a wonderful success. First, we had the delicious birthday dinner Mother had cooked and the cake and the ice cream. Then Meg and Mark gave their presents. Mark, who gets awfully good marks in manual training, had made a tie rack. He had carved it of piñon wood and polished it until it felt almost like velvet. Then, on the upright part that fastens to the wall, he had made a design of an American eagle in brass-headed nails. Running my fingers over it, I could see it just as plainly as could be. Daddy was terribly pleased. Meg had knitted him two ties that he said he would wear only on state occasions, and he tried one on because, of course, this was a state occasion, and the other one he hung over his new tie rack.

Then came my turn. I hadn't been able to eat my ice cream because I was beginning to be so worried about not remembering the different parts of the piece I was going to play. But when Daddy said in his most chuckly, smily voice, "Well, now, don't tell me Bobbie forgot me. Because if she did, she's not the friend I thought she was," right then all the worry left me. I slid out of my chair and ran around to his side of the table and gave him a big hard kiss on his cheek.

"Maybe you'll think it's a funny sort of present," I told him, "but it is something I made for you on your birthday, and it's about Perky because you gave her to me. So now, listen."

The very second my fingers touched the keys, all the parts of the piece came rushing back to me. Perky seemed to hop and dance around and chase her tail the way she often does—the little grace notes told how she did it—and then she seemed to grow tired and more tired, and at last she fell asleep.

That part I did in 3/4 time, and the end was almost a lullaby, soft, you know, ever so soft.

When I had finished, everyone clapped—that is, everyone but Daddy. He came and put his arms around me and held me close for a long minute, with his cheek against my hair. Then he whispered, "Thank you, baby, thank you so much!"

Later that evening he asked me to play it again, and this time, with all the dishes out of the way and everybody relaxed and sampling the maple fudge Meg had made, he clapped loudest of all. It was one of the happiest times I can remember.

And speaking of happy times, I think I should tell you about the concert that was postponed the day I began this book. Maybe the disappointment at not hearing it when I had expected to made it all the more exciting when I did.

Our seats were about in the middle of the concert hall so we could hear every tiniest sound and still not be too close to the orchestra where the brasses might seem too loud.

Just waiting for the music to begin was thrilling.

Everybody had been talking and rattling their programs, but suddenly they stopped. Then they began to clap and Mother whispered that the conductor had just walked to the podium. When the clapping finally stopped, there was another little bit of quiet. Everything was as still as still. Then I heard the conductor tap his baton. I held my breath, waiting. Then began the most beautiful sound I have ever heard. It was the opening bars of Tchaikovsky's "Sleeping Beauty." How can I tell you what it was like? Everybody should hear that wonderful sound. I loved it so much I sort of ached all over and I was afraid I was going to cry. I think Mother knew how I felt because she took my hand and held it tight.

That whole afternoon was like a dream. When I got home, I tried to play some of the phrases on the piano, picking them out with one finger, and that night I could not sleep for listening to the beautiful sounds that still went on and on in my mind. Someday, I kept thinking, someday perhaps I can play with a great orchestra. I'll try. Daddy brought me two records of Tchaikovsky's waltzes and I've been studying them, gradually learning to play parts of them.

I WISH every girl in the world could have a brother like Mark. Though he teases me a lot and calls me Dopey, he's never really cross, and some of the things I enjoy most I just wouldn't have if it were not for Mark.

For instance, there is the bicycle. Mark has a bike, but when he knew how much I wanted to learn to ride, he coaxed Daddy to get us a tandem. It wasn't hard to learn to ride, really. Mark rode the front seat and then, with Daddy walking beside me holding me on, I rode the back seat. We went up and down the driveway over and over again until I learned to balance myself properly. Then we went out on the road and in just a few days we were skimming along just having a ball. Now we sometimes ride to school, though I usually go with Meg because Mark enjoys riding his own bike with the other boys and I hate to be a tag-along. Just the same, we do have the nicest rides, especially when we go on a family picnic and the others ride in the car. Riding a bicycle is ever so much more fun.

Another thing Mark taught me was to run into a twirling rope and jump rope with Meg and Linda.

I had been able to jump by myself ever since I was a very little girl, but jumping when two other people were turning the rope was different, and at first I just couldn't make myself run forward and jump. I could hear the rope hit the ground with a soft little pat, and what I had to learn to do was count the beat and then jump right after the rope had hit the ground and was making its upward curve again. We had a lot of good laughs and some spills and banged into one another, but it was all fun and now I very seldom miss.

When I began this story, I spoke of the rehearsal I was supposed to have gone to and forgot. It was for the school entertainment in which everyone through Junior High took part, so Mark and I both had parts. It was a series of tableaux and songs and recitations about great people in American history. Jimmie Parks was Abraham Lincoln and recited part of the Gettysburg Address. He was good, too, and Meg said he really looked like Lincoln in his long black coat and high hat.

Linda was Molly Pitcher; and Ellen and Larry Bowman did a little skit about Daniel Boone and

his wife in the wilderness of Kentucky. That was one of the best acts, I thought, because, as they sat in front of their fire talking, you could hear Indian drums far off and you knew they were in danger. Mark had told me it was Fred and Tommy Driscomb playing the drums, but even so I thought it was wonderful the way neither Daniel nor his wife let themselves be scared—at least not showing each other they were scared. It was such a fine little story of pioneer courage that everyone applauded a long time.

Our act came a little while later, after the fourth grade sang "Santa Lucia" and three eighth-grade boys dressed in Revolutionary costumes played guitars and sang some English ballads. Mark and I were supposed to be George and Martha Washington. We wore powdered wigs and Mother had made me a pretty costume with a very full skirt and lace around the neck and elbow sleeves. We were supposed to have just come back home to Mount Vernon after Washington's second term as President, and we were so glad to be back home that Washington made this little speech to Martha—

Mark and I had rehearsed it so much that we would say it to each other almost every time we met:

George: "Well, my dear, it is good indeed to be home once more, isn't it, far from all the pomp and confusion of public life?"

Martha: "Oh, so good! Mount Vernon never looked so beautiful nor have I been so happy in many, many months. I declare I could dance for joy!"

George: "And what is to prevent that? Come, how about a minuet?"

Miss Blair, who teaches music appreciation at school, played Mozart's Minuet in F for our dance. Mark and I had rehearsed it with her many times, so we had no trouble, and when we'd finished everyone clapped and clapped and some of the big boys whistled and stamped. Maybe this was because we had tried so much to make the scene real. We didn't just stand and speak lines to each other. George would sort of chuckle when he spoke about dancing and put his arm around Martha's shoulder, and she would laugh up at him and pat his lapel.

We tried awfully hard to seem natural and I think it helped.

That entertainment meant something very special to me. It taught me that I was not nervous about performing before people, and it made me think about how young Mozart was when he wrote that lovely minuet—only six years old. The next day Daddy brought me a book about Mozart with a lot of his compositions in it. Mother read the story to me and played some of the pieces he had composed.

I cannot exactly explain it, but somehow something inside me began to make me more anxious to compose things of my own. With my stylus I pricked out the notes of several of the Mozart pieces and learned to play them. Then I set to work practicing as Miss Blair gave me longer and harder exercises. And I began trying the simple tune—with my right hand—of the piece I knew I wanted to write, a piece I was going to call "Summer Woodland."

I had been thinking about that piece for a long time because whenever we have gone on picnics 35 and have passed through little patches of woodland I can feel the difference. Even in the canyons where it is often very cool, my feet make a crunchy, gritty sound on the sandy ground, and the only birds one sees or hears are the swift roadrunners Mark always points out to me. He will say, "Bobbie, there goes a roadrunner, over there to your right, a sleek, dark little fellow with his wings folded around him like a tight jacket. Now he's gone, but can he run!" Sometimes a great golden eagle passes overhead and I think I can hear its wings. It sounds beautiful but cruel—I don't know why I think so.

But the woods are different. There the ground is soft and cool under my sneakers and it smells green and shady, and you can hear little birds twittering everywhere. Perky loves the woods, too, and I can hear her sniffling at roots as she trots ahead of me.

Those long hikes into the canyon and back home again are some of the most wonderful times our family has. We sing a lot as we walk along, and we stop often while Daddy tells us about the country all around us, the huge rocks sticking out, and the deep gorges below us. When we get home in the evening, I am always so sleepy that I go straight to bed after a glass of milk, and you cannot imagine the dreams I have—the beautiful, beautiful countries I walk through.

I don't want to miss anything I think might be interesting to other girls, sighted girls who may not quite understand certain differences between us. For instance, to me, it is always—well, daylight. I don't mean glaring light, but just a natural light in which we all live and move about. So, when people sometimes speak of the blind being always "in the dark," I don't quite understand. The only time it is dark to me is when I am asleep and do not dream. The rest of the time I "see" people and things around me as I picture them. So I am not ever lonely.

Perhaps the best way to explain how a blind person feels about seeing is this: he never has known what it is to see as sighted people think of seeing, so he does not miss it. Do you miss not being able to speak Chinese? Or living at the bottom of the sea? Or walking on your hands instead of your feet 37 if you choose to? Well, that is what sight means to me, to all of us who have never known it. Besides, as Meg said when she was a little girl and I was a baby, "Bobbie sees with her ears and fingers and toes. I wish I could."

One of the nicest things to happen to us was Cousin Grace's visit two years ago. She was nineteen years old, and the very first moment I ran my fingers over her face I knew how pretty she was. She looked a lot like Meg and she had Meg's chuckly laugh. She had come from New York because her doctor said she must live in a hot, dry climate for a while at least, and Arizona is certainly hot and dry.

I remember how excited we were waiting for the bus to come in from Canyon City and how I loved her right away, because when she kissed me and said, "Hello, Robin, I brought you something I think you'll like," she didn't say it as though she was sorry for me or thought she ought to treat me differently from the others. The "something" she had brought was a portable record player, a very fine one, Mother said, and a big carton of records.

So I owe Grace more than I can say for bringing us the glorious music of Brahms and Schumann and Mendelssohn and so many others.

Everyone loved Grace. She was so gentle and so gay all at the same time, so full of fun and yet so thoughtful. She taught me how to make cream sauce for chipped beef and how to mix and roll out and cut biscuits. After we put them in the oven, we would set the little timer and after a few trials we had delicious biscuits I'd made all by myself.

Sometimes she walked to school with me and we would stop at the store windows and Grace would tell me all about what was in them so that I could "see" them perfectly. Then, after she had been with us for quite a while, Mr. Palmer came to dinner one Sunday. Though Mr. Palmer was quite a lot younger than Daddy, he was one of his close friends; he had come to Carsonville on business for a few days. He had been at our house before and we all liked him very much. And I know he liked us, especially Grace, because he came again the next week. After that, he was with us a great deal, and soon we were all calling him Gordon.

It was Christmas time when Gordon and Grace told Daddy they wanted to be married. Goodness, but we were happy! They were both such dear people and, as Mother said, they just seemed made for each other. So we all began making plans for the wedding which would be in April, the most beautiful month out here on the desert. And guess what? Meg and I were to be Grace's bridesmaids! I could hardly believe it, but it was true.

It was hard keeping my mind on my lessons with all the excitement at home. The sewing machine whirred and whirred; I pulled bastings; and when Gordon brought Grace's engagement ring and I ran my finger over the diamond in it, I thought of icicles with the sun shining on them, white and cold.

Those were happy months. And when April came I was almost sorry, knowing the excitement would soon be over. After that Grace wouldn't be with us any more, but in a home of her own in Canyon City.

I shall never, never forget that beautiful wedding day. It was so warm that the doors and windows stood open. Meg and I wore yellow linen dresses with narrow green velvet ribbons around our waists and the same velvet ribbons around our hair. Daddy said we looked like yellow daisies. As for Grace— my goodness, she must have looked beautiful! Her dress was white organdy and her veil, which came just to her shoulders, felt like a soft cloud when I put my fingertips on it.

The roses were all in bloom, and everywhere I walked I touched big bowls of them. I had to be a little careful because the furniture in the living room had all been moved and I had to keep telling myself that it was now a long, empty room with a lot of greenery and some tall vases of white flowers in the big picture window at its end.

Gordon's father and brother had come the day before and were staying at the hotel, and that evening we had our rehearsal. It was fun and it was a little solemn, too. We had a record on the player that played Handel's beautiful Wedding Anthem sung by a great choir, and listening, I felt there just must be a real choir there, hidden in the patio perhaps. The music was easy to keep time with. First, 41

Mr. Palmer and Erich, Gordon's brother, walked in, and then, after Meg and I had counted five, we followed them. Doctor Baker and Gordon stood in the window facing us, and when Meg touched my hand, I stopped walking and we stood a little to one side to let Grace and Daddy walk through. They stopped just ahead of us.

Now came the part I had to be careful about. I wanted to do it perfectly, without a single mistake. I knew that when we had all reached the place facing the window and Doctor Baker and Gordon, the music would stop. Mark had been told just where to shut it off at the end of a measure. When it stopped, Grace would turn and hand me her bouquet. I must be careful to take it from her nicely, not grab at it or—my goodness—drop it. For the rehearsal, Grace carried a bunch of flowers from the garden and it wasn't hard to feel just where her fingers were on the stems and where mine must be when I took them from her. We went over every bit of it twice and then we were letter-perfect. That evening Daddy took us all to a wonderful dinner at the hotel, and because Mother sat beside

me and told me exactly what was on my plate, I didn't have any trouble at all and had such a good time.

The wedding was at four o'clock the next afternoon. In the dining room, Mother had put out her prettiest china—I love the plates with their fluted edges—and her best silver tableware. The shops in town called Pandora's Box sent out boxes and boxes of tiny sandwiches and little cakes and a big carton filled with little ice–cream helpings shaped like wedding bells. Mark and Meg and I were told to stay out of the kitchen, and we did, mostly, except that I did feel all the big packages of goodies and Mark sneaked me a sandwich that tasted like all the good things in the world mashed up to make a filling and put between two of the tiniest slices of bread you can imagine. When I have my wedding, I'll have Pandora's Box make my sandwiches, too.

After half–past three, people kept coming and coming and I could hear everyone laughing and talking out on the porch and in the living room. Meg and I were in Grace's room with her. Mother was outside talking to the guests. Just at four o'clock, Daddy rapped at the door and said in the voice I like best, "All ready, girls? Here we go then."

Suddenly everything was quiet outside and then the music began, and we knew that Doctor Baker and Gordon were waiting and that Mr. Palmer and Erich were walking up the living room toward them. My hands were cold, and I noticed Meg's hand was cold, too, when she touched mine as we started out of the bedroom after counting five. After that, it was easy. I knew we were in step by the way Meg's skirt swished against mine, and I remembered to keep my head high as Mother had taught me, looking ahead and smiling. Then Meg touched my hand, the music stopped, and I heard a soft swish as Grace turned to hand me her bouquet. Now was my most important moment. I held out my hands and there was the bouquet, all safe and warm from Grace's fingers. It was over. I hadn't dropped it. Handing the bouquet back to her afterward was not hard because she simply took it from me. Meanwhile there were Doctor Baker's solemn 45 words and Grace's and Gordon's answers, and in just a few moments Grace was Mrs. Gordon Palmer.

I knew how pretty she looked in her going-away suit for she had let me feel it all over and the soft silk blouse under it with a big bow at the neck. I thought her hat was sweet, too. It was just a little bandeau made of crushed flowers with a veil. She gave me a quick little hug and kiss on the porch before she and Gordon ran down to their car, and when I went back into the house I remember I felt lonely for the first time in my life. I was going to miss Grace very much.

But then you never know when something nice is just waiting for you around the corner. I was standing at the back window of the living room wishing Mark or somebody would come by. A lot of people were still there and all the furniture had been changed around and I was afraid of bumping into things if I began trying to find my way. And just then who should come up but Miss Blair.

"Ah, there you are, Bobbie," she said. "I've been looking everywhere for you. I wanted to tell you how lovely you and Meg looked at the wedding, and there is something else I want to tell you. I've been thinking you should submit your Rondo to the contest."

You see, the Canyon City Symphony Association holds a contest each year for music students who may submit their compositions, and the winning composition is played by the Canyon City Symphony Orchestra. I had been working at a little piece which I called simply Rondo. It was pretty, I thought, and I put into it my different moods: the times when I was so happy that the whole world seemed to be laughing along with me; other times when everything seemed dull, without any life or color at all; and still other times when nothing seemed right and I was close to being sad or, as Great-Grandfather Preston would have said, when I was feeling sorry for myself. I had been wanting to ask Miss Blair if she thought I'd dare submit my Rondo to the contest.

Now I could only squeeze her fingers very hard where they held mine and say, "Do you really, really think so, Miss Blair? Do you think it would have a chance?"

She laughed her pleasant little crinkly laugh that I like so much and said, "Indeed I do think it has every chance in the world. I'm going into Canyon City tomorrow and I'll stop to see the director of the orchestra and get all the information about the contest. Then we can plan. Meanwhile, work on your harmony and scales and I'll let you know what happens."

Well, that was more than two years ago. In between, I found I hadn't lost Grace after all. She and Gordon and now little Bruce come to see us often and we go to see them at their house in Canyon City. It is an up-and-down house and has a tiny fountain on its garden wall that makes a cool sound on a hot day.

Oh, I do owe dear Miss Blair so very much. She did as she promised and found out all about the contest and my Rondo was entered. Though it did not win a prize, it did win honorable mention and that made me very happy. Then last year I was too busy with my playing to give much time to composing, so I didn't enter the contest. Now, though . . . well, we'll come to that later.

If it were not for Miss Blair, I doubt that I ever would have had the patience to learn to read notes in Braille. But she brought me one lovely piece after another, played them for me, made me eager to play them as they were written, not by ear. So I learned to read music in Braille. It was not very hard, just slow. Whenever I have a new piece in Braille, I find myself grinning when I think what Mark would do if he had to learn it. I know he would stutter and fuss and try to go too fast and get all mixed up the way Perky used to when she was a puppy and got all wound up in a ball of yarn.

The way you learn to play Braille notes is to read the treble notes with your left hand while you play them with your right hand. Then you read the bass notes with your right hand and play them with your left. When you've done it over and over a good many times, you stop "reading" and use both hands to play. It takes time, but it is wonderful if you love music. Sometimes I wonder if sighted people can possibly love music as much as a blind person does. Of course, all musicians are very, very interested in perfect technique, but sometimes I think no sighted person can feel the pictures in tones that a blind person can.

For instance, when Mark and I were busy learning the steps for the minuet in the school entertainment, Mother read me stories about the days of Martha and George Washington, how the beautiful ballrooms looked, and the way Martha's pretty gown sort of swooped and dipped when she danced. I could see it all, so now when I play one of Mozart's minuets I try to put that all into my playing. I know that music is so much more than notes. It is everything you put into it with your fingers as you play, all the gaiety, all the gentleness or harshness or sadness which the notes bring to your heart.

Now that another year has passed and another contest is coming up, I am working harder than I ever have worked at anything, for I am going to enter my "Summer Woodland" and it must tell exactly what a quiet wood means to me. If I can do that, then perhaps this time I'll win something more than just honorable mention.

I N J U S T a few weeks now, school will close for the summer. I have enjoyed this year a lot and several things have made it interesting. This year, for instance, for the first time I have had to go to different rooms for different subjects. At first it confused me. I was so used to going from the front door of the building straight to my desk. Now, for history I must go up to Miss Herbert's room on the second floor, and from there to my English class downstairs again, and then around the corner and down a long hall to Miss Ordway's room. As Linda Winthrup takes most of my subjects, we walked together at first, but after a few days I made her let me find my way alone though she walked behind me. I made a few mistakes. Once, I bumped into a big boy who yelled, "Whoops, baby. Make way for the Marines!" and once I got all turned around and started into the science lab. But in just a little while I got the knack of it and could hurry from one class to another with the other girls and boys. This taught me to figure out other directions, so now I can find my way almost anywhere in the building without getting lost.

It is hard for me sometimes to listen to other girls say ugly things about their mothers, because Meg and Mark and I think there is no one in the whole world quite as wonderful as Mother. What would we do without her? Not a day passes that she doesn't teach me something important—something especially important for a blind person to know. For instance, of course she has taught me the really important things—like trusting God and being honest and kind, things like that, you know. But she has shown me so many things that maybe not all blind people know about. So I'll write them down here, and if, perhaps, some blind girl reads about them, they will help her, too.

When I am in a strange room and someone asks me to sit down and puts a chair near me, I do not stoop and run my hand over the seat to make sure just how high it is. That would look awkward and just call attention to the fact that I am blind. Instead, Mother has taught me to stand beside the chair for a second and feel with my leg how high or low the seat is and then just sit down as anyone else would do.

Another thing: at table she has taught me never to make any quick or sudden movements with my hands. I slowly run my fingers up and over the edge of the table and locate my napkin and water glass. Now I know exactly where the glass is when I want to reach for a drink. In the same way, I slowly locate the knives and forks and the butter spreader if there is one.

About the food on my plate: when I am visiting anyone, I ask whoever sits beside me what is on the plate—at home, of course, I know. Then, with my fork, I locate everything on the plate—meat, potato, and usually another vegetable—and it is not hard then to eat just like a sighted person. Naturally, sometimes there are accidents. A slippery piece of asparagus can slide off your fork and land smack on your nice clean blouse; a lettuce leaf sometimes dribbles. But that doesn't happen often. When it does, Mother says the best thing to do is try not to be embarrassed but just say "I'm sorry," and then go on with my meal. Walking is another thing. She has told me how unhappy some blind people look because, so often when they walk along, 53 they keep their heads bowed. She said—and I'll never forget it—"Remember, Bobbie, life is ahead of us, not on the ground under our feet. So walk toward it, not over it. Hold your head high as God intended you to." Those are just a few of the important things Mother has taught me, and I could go on and on.

This past weekend we had the most marvelous hike down into the Grand Canyon. Sometimes the wind, all warm and smelling of the mountainsides, came blowing up to us. It sounded like music from forgotten places. Mark and Daddy made a fire and we all cooked our hot dogs on the ends of sticks. Were they ever good!

But I think the best hike I've ever known was the one we took back in April when we hiked ten miles into Havasu Canyon where the Havasupi Indians live. This was an overnight hike, so we carried bedrolls and slept on the ground near Havasu Creek. The only way you can get there is by pack horse or on foot. We went on foot, and Perky led me all the way and I never made a single misstep. If you have never slept in a canyon, you cannot imagine how still it is. All of a sudden some coyote would howl in the night, the wildest, saddest sound I have ever heard. Then it was still again, still as if the world were holding its breath. I loved that hike. Someday maybe I'll put it into music.

Vacation has flown by so this year that I just cannot believe it is almost over. I guess that is because I have been so busy working on my piece for the contest, and now at last it is finished. I have changed and changed parts of it, but now Miss Blair will not let me make any more changes. She says that if you go on making too many changes in any work, you end up by spoiling it. She says I have reached my "point of achievement," as she calls it, and now I must be satisfied. This morning I slipped "Summer Woodland" into a big manila envelope Daddy had brought me, said a little prayer for it, and put it in the mailbox.

No one knows what it will mean to me if it should win first place. You see, the other winners all are mentioned on the program, but only the prize-winning composition gets played by the orchestra. And meanwhile I am beginning to hope for something else, something I am not going to even write about here in my book until I think I have a chance of making it happen. I believe if you want something that is really good, not just some silly thing like a million dollars or a castle built of glass, and if you do your part by working toward it and praying for it and never doubting that you'll get it, you probably will. So that is what I'm doing now that "Summer Woodland" is finished. In a little while I'll write about it, but not just yet.

The high point of last week was the church fair. Linda and I had finished our afghan blocks and Mother showed us how to sew them together. Then we took turns crocheting the border that went around it. It wasn't as hard as we thought it might be, for Linda tried to crochet more loosely and I tightened up my loose stitches as we went along. In the end the afghan was a big success and everyone said how pretty it was. The best part, though, was that it made fifty-two dollars for the library fund; and, added to that, it was won by one of the very dearest old ladies, Mrs. Pickard, whose husband teaches at one of the reservations. So Linda and I were happy. We plan to make another one next year.

Our church fairs always close with a little entertainment, and this year Meg and Mark and I sang a little French trio and did the country dance that went with it. It was called "Allons au bord de la mer" which means "Let's go to the seashore," and we had a lot of fun doing it. The dance is a sort of hopping, skipping, round-and-round dance, and at home when we practiced it, we always got to laughing because Mark once yelled at the end of the dance, "And now I'll dunk you in the drink." But it went off very well at the fair, and everyone clapped and clapped until we sang it again.

I keep forgetting to tell you about what we call our "family nights." We try to have them once a week, usually on Friday, because on Friday evening you never feel hurried. On family night, we talk over the things that have perhaps bothered us during the week, things we're not quite sure how to handle: like the time Mark saw Fred Martin take Mr. Stewart's fountain pen off his desk; or another time when Meg wanted to go to spend two weeks in Denver and Daddy had to explain how expensive the braces for her teeth had been; or last year when I thought I wanted to learn the flute. Sometimes we bring things we've heard about or read that we don't understand, or exciting, lovely things we want to talk about some more, or a joke we want to tell.

This last family night—last night—all I could talk about was the contest. In my whole life I have never wanted anything so much as to hear my composition played by an orchestra. I kept wondering if I had the harmony right. Should I have made more changes? The best thing about the contest, I think, is that the judges never know whose composition they are judging until they have finally made their choice. You see, every composition is given a number when it comes in; you must not write your name on your composition but on a separate sheet of paper. Then the number of your composition is put on the paper beside your name and that goes to someone outside the orchestra. In that way, the competition is always fair. No one 58 can play favorites.

I got so excited talking about it that I guess Mark understood even better than Mother or Daddy or Meg just how I felt, because he said something I am going to remember always. He said, "Bobbie, maybe you'll win and maybe you won't, but try to look at it this way—the way my chemistry teacher looks at things. He says many a laboratory test fails in spite of the most careful work, but that isn't the important thing. The important thing is the work, the effort, that went into it. You've probably learned more in the weeks you've been working on 'Summer Woodland' than you learned in a year or even more. You've gained an awful lot. Remember that, no matter how the contest goes. Will you try?"

Yes, I'll try, but oh, my goodness! School opens Monday, beginning my last year in Junior High. I wonder whether a year from today I'll be any closer to my new big wish than I am today. Tomorrow I am going to listen to records at the record store and Mother says I may buy one that I really love. I'm pretty sure it will be a Chopin concerto.

I REMEMBER that when I began writing in this book I thought I'd be writing every day, but the past two weeks have been so full that there has not been time for anything but what filled each day. Every time I think of those two weeks I find myself thinking of a pyramid. The bottom part was going back to school and meeting new kids and getting new assignments, meeting new teachers. A lot of new Braille books have come in, which is wonderful, and at first I thought I'd sign up for the class play. Then, because my new plan may keep me so busy, I thought I'd better not. And every day I'd come tearing home, hoping against hope that Mother would say I had a letter from the orchestra about "Summer Woodland." It was hard not to show how disappointed I was when nothing came, and I began to tell myself that my "laboratory test" had failed.

Then I'd remind myself that the effort that had gone into it was the important part. That was easy to say but hard to take when all your effort did not seem to do much for you. I really did try hard, though, not to let the family know how worried I was because it is terrible to be with someone who is worried and not be able to do anything to help. And what could they do? Mark made me go on long rides with him on our tandem after school, and we sang my favorite "Greensleeves" as we spun along until finally we had worked it into a duet. I knew why he was doing it and why Meg told so many funny stories about things that happened at the tennis courts. Mother and Daddy just went along as though we weren't all pretty nervous, but I knew they understood.

We were having supper Tuesday evening when the telephone rang and, because Meg was expecting a call from one of the girls, she answered it. I heard her say, "No, this is Meg Preston. Yes, Robin's here. Just a moment." Then she turned away from the phone and said, "It's for you, Bobbie," and I think for just a second my heart stopped beating. Could it—*could it be?* I slid out of my chair and went to the telephone and took the receiver from Meg's fingers.

I don't know why, but I couldn't make my voice sound as I wanted it to when I said "Hello?" I waited a second and then a pleasant voice, a woman's, said, "Is this Robin Preston?" I hope I said it was, but all I can remember is that I nodded. Then the voice said, "Robin, I am speaking for the Canyon City Symphony Orchestra and I am happy to tell you that your composition, 'Summer Woodland,' has been chosen by the judges as the best submitted in the contest. It will be played by the orchestra on October the tenth. Meanwhile, you will receive a covering letter from us. Congratulations, Robin."

My arms and legs felt cold all of a sudden. I almost dropped the receiver. Instead of saying any of the polite things I should have, I just began shouting, "Oh, thank you—thank you—thank you—thank you!" and hung up. Then I began to cry so hard that it scared me. I couldn't stop and I even forgot my way back to the table and walked smack into the kitchen wall instead, and banged myself hard. Daddy came and put his arms around me and held me close, and pretty soon I began to stop shaking and felt warm again and terribly ashamed of making such a goose of myself. *But it had hap-*

pened—I had actually won! It was like walking through gold-colored clouds, your feet never touching anything, and coming from all around you great waves of the most glorious music in heaven or earth. I just felt as though I couldn't hold all the happiness and thanksgiving I knew was in my heart. It is silly to try to describe it so I won't, but I know the very tiptoe point of the week's pyramid was that telephone call.

Of course, I telephoned Miss Blair right away to tell her about my winning the contest. She said, "I'm as happy as you are about this, Robin, and I am coming in to see you tomorrow to talk to you about something important. I'll be there about four if that is convenient for your mother, because I must speak to her, too."

I couldn't keep my mind on my classes Wednesday and made some bad mistakes in arithmetic. Mr. Bryant, the math teacher, said, "Robin, you're wool-gathering today. Now put your mind on your work and stop dreaming."

I knew he was right because I was dreaming. The 10th of October was not so very far off; and, besides that, what did Miss Blair want to talk to Mother and me about?

Mother had made tea; and when I heard Miss Blair's car drive up, I knew how nice the living room looked, with the pretty tea things and Mother wearing the dress I like so much, the one that feels like kitten fur. I had changed to my best new yellow sweater, too, so it really was a party.

Miss Blair did something when she came in that she had never done before: she came straight to me and kissed my cheek. And she said a lovely thing. She said, "Robin, great doors are swinging open for you. If you work hard, you can pass through them into a whole new world, and I know you can do it." We talked about the contest and the concert when "Summer Woodland" was to be played. And then, when Mother had poured her second cup of tea and I'd passed the sponge cake, Miss Blair said, "Now let's talk about what I really came for, shall we? I think it's time for Robin's recital."

It is silly, I know, but when I grow excited, my hands and my nose get cold, and now I felt as though I was running in a cold wind. I wasn't sure I understood. I was remembering that two years ago a German boy named Rudolph Weingarten had had a recital and then he had gone back to Germany and played there with orchestras, and in England, too. Now Miss Blair was talking about my recital. Could she mean she was giving me a recital all my own? I tried hard to listen, to take it in, but all my thinking got mixed up. I kept hearing bits of the piece I'd been working on, wondering how they would sound at a concert, how I'd manage the hard part in that Beethoven sonata. It was all jumbled up in my mind. Then I heard Mother saying, "Robin, Miss Blair is speaking to you," and I woke up. She was saying, "You are ready for your recital now, Robin. If you, too, feel that you are ready, we'll decide on our program. What do you say?"

She put her hand over mine and her voice had said so much more than came out in the words that I knew I, too, wanted to say much more than I could find the right words for. All I could say was, "It is so wonderful! I'll try my best, Miss Blair." I think Miss Blair understood because she   65 gave my fingers an extra squeeze. After she had gone, I put Perky's leash on her and we walked round and round the block until at last I felt quiet again. At supper, nobody said very much and I knew we all were thinking the same thing: how much had happened in just two days.

That was Wednesday and now it is Saturday and I've spent every second I could practicing. Especially I've worked on the stretching exercises to help me reach octaves without slurring. And I'll tell you a little secret. When I get tired, I play things that are just fun, things like "That Old Man" and some of the tunes from the picture *Mary Poppins,* and then I go back to work feeling all fresh and rested. This morning when Mark and I went over to Grandpa's he was just as excited as the rest of the family about both the contest and the concert and promised he was going to think up a new kind of cookie and call it "Robin's Recital Cookie."

I JUST had to put a date at the top of this page!
Yesterday was the day of the contest concert
and I still tingle all over just thinking about it. We
all went together—Mother, Daddy, Meg, Mark,
and I. And then just before the concert started,
someone patted my shoulder and whispered, "Hi,
Childie," and I knew Grandpa had come. He is the
only person who calls me "Childie" and there he
was. I just had time to reach my fingers up to
cover his for a second before everyone began to
applaud and I knew that the conductor of the
orchestra, Mr. Tate, had come to the podium. Mr.
Tate is a great conductor, but he does much more
than just conduct. He knows how to show kids the
beauty in music, beauty they might miss if he had
not told them about it before it was played. After
he has told you what each part of a piece means,
what the composer put into it when he wrote it—
then, when you hear it played, you *feel* it and you
see pictures of its meaning. It must be wonderful
to be able to do what Mr. Tate does with music.

Now all I could do was listen until the last tiny   67

bit of sound had left the concert hall and every-thing was still. Then—bang!—began one of the Slavonic Dances. My, but it was stirring. When it was over, Mark said, "Gee, I wanted to stand up and yell." So did I, almost, except that I could not get my mind off my "Summer Woodland," and my hands were getting cold and so was the tip of my nose. Another piece followed the Slavonic Dance, a march by Berlioz, but I was almost too excited to listen, and when it was over, I had to clench my hands into fists at my sides and bite my lips to keep from shaking.

Then Mr. Tate was speaking. I heard my name and the words, "Summer Woodland," and then a lot of clapping and quiet again. Just quiet. Then softly, softly, there it was—my "Summer Wood-land"! Only I almost screamed, "That's wrong!" because the orchestra was playing it in G and I had written it in C. But nobody else knew that, so it really didn't matter. The orchestra had made it into the loveliest piece. In the part where the little brook runs through the woods, the violins and cellos brought in the soft music of wind through the trees. Honestly, I do think it made a picture of a beautiful forest on a summer day just the way I've always dreamed it. After the people had stopped clapping, Daddy walked up to the platform with me and I bowed and they clapped harder and longer. Then it was over. When I went back to my seat beside Mark, he said, "La di da di da—your slip shows." If we'd been at home, I'd have mussed his hair—that makes him wild—but I couldn't right there in the concert hall. Besides, I knew my slip didn't show and that he was just being smart to hide his real feelings, so I said, "Thank you, Mark, dear, for telling me." Mother shushed us for Mr. Tate was speaking again, and in a minute we were all out in the lobby and everyone was shaking hands and saying nice things and the wonderful day was over.

Mother and I went backstage to thank Mr. Tate and as many of the members of the orchestra as were there, and Mr. Tate gave me the score of "Summer Woodland"—someday maybe I can have a recording made of it. I still cannot believe that wonderful day is over and that I have heard my own composition played by a big, important orchestra.

After I went to bed last night, I was too happy and excited to sleep and I began wondering what it is that makes you happy or unhappy, peaceful like my forest, or riled up and mad, and I know now what it is. It is all just the way you think. You could be awfully happy, for instance, the way I was about the contest, and yet you could suddenly think that maybe you'd never compose another good piece, and all your happiness would get cloudy, and pretty soon you'd forget the wonderful thing that had made you so full of joy. I promised myself I'd remember that.

I JUST looked back to see when I had written the last page and I cannot believe it was way back in October. So much has happened since then. First of all, I began my swimming lessons right after the contest concert. At first I didn't think I would like swimming because I was always afraid of having the water go over my head and then not being able to breathe. But Miss Fletcher, the teacher, taught me not to be afraid and to breathe properly, and now I can swim about as well as Meg. Also, I have had two diving lessons. I swim twice a week and I'm going to try to be as good a swimmer as Meg is a tennis player. Wouldn't it be funny if someday I won a swimming contest? You never can tell. I just love swimming.

Then there was Christmas. It was such a happy Christmas this year because Grace and Gordon and little Bruce came to spend it with us. There was the prickly, sweet-smelling tree with its long strings of smooth balls like big beads, and beautiful Christmas records on the player, and a big turkey, and mince pie. There were lots of gifts, too, for everyone. I think the one I liked most was the fine pigskin case Mother and Daddy gave me to carry my Braille books in. They are heavy, you know, and a good sturdy case makes a big difference.

But even while I was getting ready for Christmas, I was busy preparing for the recital. Miss Blair had decided on January 27 for that. We went over some of the things I had been studying and then chose some new ones, and at last the program was ready: six pieces and two possible encores. My, but I worked! Sometimes at night I'd wake myself up doing hand-stretching exercises; and every time I went to the piano, I played a bit to see if I could interpret it a little differently. I did not want the slightest thing to be wrong with anything I played at the recital. Everything had to be perfect.

By the 13th of January—my birthday, my thirteenth—I knew every note of the recital perfectly, knew just what to do with each piece to bring out its greatest beauty. My lovely new white crepe de chine dress with the soft pink bodice and cascade of pink rosebuds down the skirt was hanging in the closet. I had never been so happy.

We were at the table talking about how pretty the birthday cake was that Mother had baked when I sneezed. Then I sneezed some more and my head began to ache, and when I woke in the morning, I was too sick to think of anything—*even the recital!* Though I didn't know this until much later, Doctor Johnson came and came and came and all he could say was, "You never know about Asian flu." 73

I was learning a lot about it though: how you burned up one minute and shivered the next; how you longed for something to eat and then turned sick when you saw it. Oh, I learned a lot. Then, on a sunny morning, I woke up out of an ugly dream and was really hungry and wanted a bath. And—why I don't know—I wanted more than anything on earth to hear the record of Tchaikovsky's *Fifth Symphony*. To me it stood for getting better, for going on to what one had to do. Daddy put it on the player and, listening to it, I fell asleep again and woke up a long time afterward, feeling all well and warm and happy and anxious to practice.

Though I was sick in bed for only five days, when I got up my legs felt like rubber and when I sat down at the piano, my fingers didn't want to stretch and, most horrible of all, I couldn't remember parts of the Chopin Nocturne in E flat, which is one of my favorite pieces. Of all the pieces on the recital program, it was the one I had worked over hardest, the one Miss Blair was most pleased with. Now, suddenly, I couldn't remember the notes after the opening bars. I tried over and over again, but they wouldn't come. I didn't want Mother to hear me stumbling because I knew how she would worry for me. I just didn't know what to do. I practiced the rest of the program and it all went well, but as soon as I went back to the Nocturne, everything went blank. I kept on trying.

A whole day passed. Mark came by once and stood beside me for a moment and then went out again without, I thought, ever knowing how scared I was. At dinner that evening, we all talked about the visit Meg wanted to pay during the spring holiday to that friend of hers in Denver, and I hoped no one was thinking, as I was, that the recital was one day less than a week away and that I had forgotten the notes of my most important piece. When at last I went to bed, I ached so all over that I could not sleep, and all I could think of was a huge pudding made of notes all stirred by an enormous eggbeater and getting lumpier and lumpier. I began to wish the recital hall would burn down or that we'd have an earthquake.

The next day was Saturday, cleanup day, and as

soon as I had changed the sheets on my bed, I went into the living room thinking I would try once more to find my way to the right notes of the Nocturne. Meg had driven in to the market with Mother, and Mark was in the garage oiling his bike. I was sitting on the piano bench, trying to think what to play first, when the back door banged open and Mark came in. I could hear him in the kitchen and then he came to the living-room door. "Aren't there any more cookies?" he said and then, before I could answer, he came across the room and slid down on the bench beside me. "How's about giving our old mazurka a whirl? We haven't done it for ages. Come on."

He was already running his fingers over the keys, singing. "Tum-ti-tum, tum-tum-ti-tum," and when he reached the right beat, I began the treble part and off we went, skimming along over the piece we both loved. We finished with a flourish, laughing because it had gone so well and we were both so thrilled about it. We played again and then again, forgetting everything but the fun we were having.

Then Mark said, "Hi, play that Chopin thing

you're playing at the recital. You know—the one that goes..." He picked out the opening bars of the Nocturne and a few notes more and, without even thinking, I began playing. I'd forgotten the recital, forgotten that I had ever had any trouble with those notes. I was just playing naturally as I always had. It wasn't until I had finished the piece and let my hands just rest on the keys a second that I realized what I had done. I had played it! Some little door in my memory had swung open and I remembered it all as though I never had forgotten it. How was it possible? What was the secret? Was it because I was just relaxed and having fun and not thinking? Had Mark planned it that way? Mark—my brother Mark?

I hadn't a chance even to speak of it because he went into the kitchen again, calling over his shoulder at the door, "Keep on with me, Miss Preston, and someday maybe you'll learn how to play the piano."

The night of the recital was bitter cold and I wondered if anyone would want to come. My dress felt smooth and soft, and I had brushed my hair 77 hard to make it curl up, and Meg said I looked all right. When we left for the hall, I felt comfortable inside. We got there very early so that I could learn to walk out on the stage and to the piano without making any mistakes. It was easy. Aside from the piano being bigger than ours at home, everything was the same, so I wasn't nervous. The little waiting room offstage was warm and cozy, and soon Miss Blair and Mother were chatting and laughing just as though they were at home in our living room. You could almost forget you were in a concert hall—that it was my recital night.

I really tried not to think of it for my fingers had to stay warm. Just a few minutes before it was time to start, Mark opened the door and said, "Hi, Bobbie, I thought you'd like to know that every seat is taken. Grandpa came with Gordon and Grace and . . . " He didn't finish and I wondered a little. Afterward I knew why. Then Miss Blair put her arm around my shoulder and said, "Now, Robin. Just play as you always do for me at the studio and everything will be splendid. Good 78 luck, dear!" We walked out into the wings, and when she gave me a tiny push and said, "Now," I walked out on the stage.

For a second I could not understand the swish of sound that came up to me, and then I realized it was the audience clapping. That seemed friendly, so when I sat down at the piano, I kept thinking of our living room and of Mother and Daddy and the rest sitting there waiting for me to play, and the last bit of flutters left my stomach and my fingers were warm.

The first piece was "Le Secret" by Gautier. I always loved playing that, so it went well. After that came "The Swan" by Saint-Saëns, and then Mendelssohn's "Spinning Song." Miss Blair had always told me never to hurry with my playing, to remember that every note had its own little message, and I tried not to forget. At the end of each piece I was to count slowly to twenty before beginning the next one, and then, after I had played the first three numbers, I was to stand up, make a bow to the audience and walk off for the ten-minute intermission.

Thinking about it now, I know that as I played

each piece I felt my fingers getting stronger and the happiness inside me growing until I wanted to sing along with the notes I was playing. It was the most wonderful feeling I ever have had. I could hear Miss Blair saying: "Great doors are swinging open for you, Robin. If you work hard, you can pass through them into a whole new world." And now I could feel them beginning to swing open. Some of my happiness must have run down into the audience because when I'd finished the "Spinning Song," the applause that came up sounded like a huge rushing waterfall. They were happy, too, I could tell.

The second half of the program was much harder, at least it had been harder for me to get perfect, and I said a prayer that I'd be able to play it well. The first piece was the French Suite No. 4 in E flat major by Bach, and it went well though I was afraid, as I finished it, that I might have hurried. And I may have counted more than twenty before I began the second number. It was the Chopin Nocturne I had forgotten when I was sick. Each time I had played it since then, I had felt all that terrible fear come over me again. I tried to think of other things: Perky scratching her ear, rain splattering on the garage roof, Mark sitting beside me on the piano bench. I counted to twenty —to twenty and held my breath. I wondered if Mark, down there in the first row where he said the family would be, was suddenly as scared as I was. I tried not to think at all and began the opening bars. Now—now—*what* came next? Yes—yes! there it was, the notes rolling on, my fingers growing warmer again, the happiness coming back. I was safe! I was playing! The Nocturne sounded almost too beautiful to be real to me as I played it. I don't mean that my playing of it was beautiful but that it sang such wonderful, wonderful harmonies to me as I played. I was almost afraid I was going to cry. When I had finished, a funny sound came up from the audience, a kind of sigh.

For the last piece on the program, we had decided the Prelude in C sharp minor by Rachmaninoff would be good. It had been difficult but I liked it so much that I had not minded the work it took. I loved playing it so much that I was sorry when I

came to the end and I guess I sat for a second or two thinking how I'd like to begin all over again. Then I remembered I must stand and bow. The recital was over. But—how can I make you hear what happened then? I could not believe it. Everybody was shouting and clapping and people were calling, "Bravo! Bravo! Bravo, Robin Preston!" and Miss Blair came and took my hand and we walked two paces forward and the noise got louder and louder. Then I think Miss Blair must have held up her hand, for all the clapping and shouting stopped suddenly. I heard her say, "You have been most kind, most generous in your applause, and Robin and I do appreciate it deeply. She will now, as a token of her appreciation, play for you 'Liebestraume' by Franz Liszt."

When I had finished, the noise started all over again, and I bowed and bowed to let everyone know I was glad to have pleased them so much. At last I heard Miss Blair's little wooden clapper, the signal that I was to walk off. I was so excited that I guess I forgot all the rules and I waved—mostly to Mark. But no one seemed to mind and Miss Blair was laughing when she took my hand and said, "Oh, Robin, Robin, what a glorious evening!"

The little waiting room—dressing room, I guess it was—was already full of people when we got there and a lot of people talked to me whose voices I never had heard before.

All the family, especially Mother, seemed to know just how I felt all of a sudden, limp and tired and wanting to be somewhere where it was quiet, and they did not stay in the room. Only Mother, as she was leaving, whispered, "My blessed lambkin," and squeezed my hand. As she went out to join the others in the wings, someone else came in and everyone seemed to stop talking at once as I heard Miss Blair say, "Mr. Tate, how nice to see you."

Mr. Tate! Now I knew why someone, Mother probably, had stopped Mark from telling me before the recital started that Mr. Tate was in the audience. I should have been petrified. Now here he was, holding my hand, saying things I shall never forget: that God had given me rich gifts, that I could use them to make the world more beautiful....

Oh, so many wonderful things. I tried to thank him, but I just could not find the right words. Only I did manage to tell him how much I owed to Miss Blair, and I'm glad I did because without Miss Blair I wouldn't have had the recital in the first place.

It wasn't really very late when we got home. Gordon and Grace had dropped Grandpa on their way into Canyon City, so at last we were alone—Mother and Daddy, Meg, Mark, and I. Mother made cocoa and we just sat around and talked while we enjoyed it, and at last it was bedtime. The great day was over. As Mark said when he carried his empty cup into the kitchen and turned out the light, "It was a blast all right!"

I BEGAN this book almost two years ago, wondering how I should ever find anything interesting to write about. Now the days are so full of interesting things that there isn't time to write about them all.

Today is my fourteenth birthday. A year ago I   85

was just beginning to have the flu and the recital was just two weeks away. The time since then has been the happiest of my life. For one thing, I'm a High School freshman now and on the debating team. But that is nothing compared to the glorious time I have been having with my piano. I am trying new forms, new arrangements, and I've been spending every moment I could outside of school practicing.

Last year, I remember, I wrote in my book that whether you were happy or unhappy depended a lot upon your thinking. Today, I am looking at that page and I still believe that. For if I let myself think too much about a new thing that has come into my life, I could grow frightened and all the great joy of the past few months would evaporate like rain after a shower. Miss Blair and Mother and Daddy have been talking a lot and I hear them mention places like Chicago and New York and I know what they mean, though I pretend not to listen.

I will not let anything spoil the most wonderful thing that has ever happened to me—the thing I have dreamed about. It happened just a week ago.

86

Last week—Tuesday, it was—Mother put an envelope in my hands when I came from school.

"It's from the Symphony Orchestra, dear, addressed to you," she said. "Shall I read it to you?"

I wasn't surprised because I knew it was time for the announcements of the Children's Concert Series to be sent out, so I took off my galoshes and hung up my coat and said "Please" over my shoulder. I heard Mother slit the envelope, wondering why she didn't say anything but still thinking perhaps she was reading the program. Then, in a voice not quite like Mother's, she said, "Darling, listen to this!"

I found the couch and sat down, not really believing what I heard. It was an invitation to play with the Symphony Orchestra at one of their spring concerts, probably in April. What do you think—what do you say when anything so wonderful comes to you? All I could do was twist a button on the couch cushion and whisper over and over again, "Oh, God, thank you, God—thank you, God!"

We are not quite sure, but I shall probably play either the Beethoven *Third Piano Concerto* or Mendelssohn's *First*. I love them both. Now I can wait and dream, knowing that dreams do come true.

Great doors *have* swung open and I'm not afraid to "pass through them into a whole new world." If that world means new faraway places, I'll not spoil the happiness they may hold by thinking them strange. I'll just give them my best music and they'll not seem strange long, because wherever there is music, that is home for me.